The Garden Project

for Richard Goodman
—M. M.

SIMON SPOTLIGHT
An imprint of Simon & Schuster Children's Publishing Division
1230 Avenue of the Americas, New York, NY 10020
This Simon Spotlight edition December 2021
First Aladdin Paperbacks edition June 2010
Text copyright © 2010 by Margaret McNamara
Illustrations copyright © 2010 by Mike Gordon
All rights reserved, including the right of reproduction in whole or in part in any form.
SIMON SPOTLIGHT, READY-TO-READ, and colophon are registered trademarks of
Simon & Schuster, Inc.
For information about special discounts for bulk purchases, please contact Simon &
Schuster Special Sales at 1-866-506-1949 or business@simonandschuster.com.
Manufactured in the United States of America 1021 LAK
2 4 6 8 10 9 7 5 3 1
Cataloging-in-Publication Data was previously supplied for the paperback edition of this
title from the Library of Congress.
ISBN 978-1-5344-9895-2 (hc)
ISBN 978-1-4169-9171-7 (pbk)
ISBN 978-1-4814-6854-1 (ebook)

The Garden Project

written by Margaret McNamara
illustrated by Mike Gordon

Ready-to-Read

Simon Spotlight
New York   London   Toronto   Sydney   New Delhi

The sandbox
at Robin Hill School
was old.
"We can make it into a
garden," said Mrs. Connor.

Parents filled the sandbox
with dark brown dirt.

Mrs. Connor divided
the garden
into four squares.

"Four students
for every square."

Nick, Katie, Emma,
and Eigen
planted radish seeds.

Nick made holes in the dirt
with his fingers.

Emma dropped one seed
in each hole.
Eigen covered them up.

Becky, Hannah, Jamie,
and Michael
planted sunflower seeds.

"Just three or four,"
    said Mrs. Connor.
"Sunflowers are big."
"And they need a lot of sun!"
    said Jamie.

Andrew, Ayanna, Griffin,
and Reza
planted pea pods.

And Neil, Nia, James,
and Megan
planted lettuce.

"Yuck," said Neil. "I do not like vegetables."

"We shall see,"
said Mrs. Connor.

Every day
the first graders
tended their garden.

They watered.
They waited.
After one week
tiny green sprouts came up.

The class picked weeds.
They kept birds away.

They watered some more.
They waited some more.

After three weeks,
little lettuces were growing.

"They are so cute!" said Nia.

After four weeks,
the sunflowers were starting
to grow taller.

"Taller than me!"
said Hannah.

At last the first-grade garden
was ready to harvest.

Mrs. Connor made
lettuce and radish salad,
with pea pods on top.

"Yummy!" said Neil.

"Yes," said Becky.
   She bit into a pea pod.
"It tastes just like sunshine."